DREAM BiG DREAMS

An Inspirational Children's Bedtime Story

Written by
Zander Bingham

Illustrated by
Sian Rips

GREEN RHINO
MEDIA

First Printing: August 2021

Green Rhino Media LLC

228 Park Ave S #15958

New York, NY 10003-1502

United States of America

www.greenrhinomedia.com

ISBN 978-1-949247-24-4 (Paperback - US)

ISBN 978-1-949247-23-7 (Hardcover - US)
ISBN 978-1-949247-27-5 (eBook - US)
ISBN 978-1-949247-28-2 (Paperback - UK/AU)
ISBN 978-1-949247-29-9 (Hardcover - UK/AU)
ISBN 978-1-949247-30-5 (eBook - UK/AU)

Library of Congress Control Number: 2020924467

For Cedar and Saylor

This wondrous day began at dawn,
now it's ending as we yawn.

We grew a bit, we're older too,
learned something new, we always do.

We've adventured, played, laughed, and cried —
life can be such a wild ride.

Memories of all we did and said,
float round and round inside our heads.

Read a book and snuggle in,
smile a happy, sleepy grin.

Now we're calm and tucked in tight,
breathe in deep, turn out the light.

As we sleep, the dreams begin, some are moments relived again.

Other times they're something new—far-off lands or creatures blue.

Dream big dreams of marvelous things,
skip or run, or soar with wings.

Travel to places high and low, climb up mountains, dance in snow.
A bustling city, an ancient tree, perhaps a village by the sea.

Stars above bring joy and wonder, go explore them while you slumber.
Don't let gravity hold you down, there's lots more fun still to be found.

Take a rocket to the moon,
next stop Mars, be there soon!

As you zoom past Saturn's rings, set your mind to bigger things.
The universe may know no bounds, oh-so much remains unfound.

Sometimes the most amazing places are the ones we find in cozy spaces, where loving arms and friendly faces cuddle us close in warm embraces.

Dream you're a poet, an inventor, or painter,
share your talents and become a creator.

For what the world needs, more than ever, are people who are strong and clever, people who will do whatever, whatever they can to make it better.

Be resilient, be outstanding,
even when it seems confounding.

For sometimes answers may not follow,
but maybe they will come tomorrow.

Dream big dreams of little things, of bigger things...

and the in between.

Dream unbound, dream aloud,
dream of futures to be found.

The world belongs to those who dream,
those who search for things unseen.

And when this night becomes a new day,
start making and creating, *doing* is the way!

Show how brilliant life can be, dream big dreams for you and me.
Dream big dreams the whole world can see.

Good night, sleep tight.

About the Author

Zander Bingham was born and raised on a boat.
It was captured by pirates when he was just 12 years old. He, along with his family and crew, swam to a nearby island where Zander spent his days imagining swashbuckling adventures on the high seas.

Well, not exactly.

But Zander did love boating adventures as a kid. And he always dreamed of exploring deserted islands and being a real-life castaway. He grew up cruising around Australia, the USA, and The Bahamas.

He eventually captained his very own sailboat, living aboard and exploring the Adriatic Sea with his family. His thirst for exploration, his positive and encouraging nature, and his new-found passion for writing stories to read to his boys at bedtime, led to the creation of Dream Big Dreams.

He has also written a children's adventure series called Jack Jones and has several other exciting projects in the works as well.

Zander Bingham lives with his wife, two young, energetic boys, and lots and lots of LEGO.

www.zanderbingham.com

Made in the USA
Coppell, TX
03 November 2021